andsome s arah ares

Word rh
Big clout
hez out
Whos bout
whata lout
water spout
don't shout
make a pout
Oot you Lout

essence—
quintessence
in evidence
other presence—
hosted plant

Portuguise
thats twice
run mice
wonder thrice
Back Heist
Niedo fliece

Nebo koveza
Amanda Henen
giver such pleasure
take her measure
in Your leasure

Never fib
Baby crib
womens lib
Lama bib
Got dibs

double knot
why not
wet spot
so hot
fox trot
nazie lot
ink blot
dark plot
Not a lot
Tittle a Jot
This hot blast

a man play
Amy hay
ride a sleigh
bale some hay
peter fay
what du weigh
months of may
wanna say hey
Slms of Ray
on Pine Key
dont delay
Voltier Kay   C2
Mamm Flag   double play — say Hay!

Startswith—
end, with

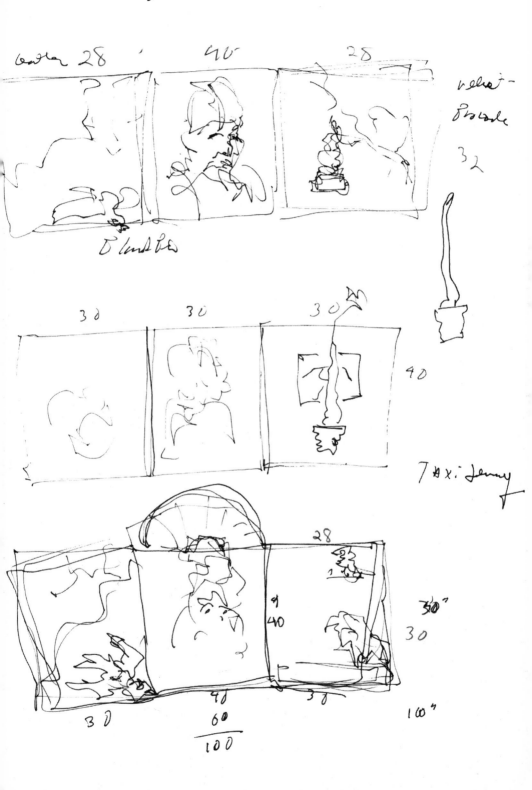

Also by William Dunlap

DUNLAP

HOMECOMINGS

With Willie Morris

SHORT
MEAN
FICTION

Words and Pictures

William Dunlap

*For Matn & Kos —
and all our Mississippien.
Best Billi Dunb*

NAUTILUS PRESS

ISBN: 978-1-936-946-70-9
The Nautilus Publishing Company
426 South Lamar Blvd., Suite 16
Oxford, Mississippi 38655
Tel: 662-513-0159
www.nautiluspublishing.com
www.williamdunlap.com
First Edition.
Cover and interior design by John Langston
Printed in Canada

Library of Congress Cataloging-in-Publication Data
has been applied for.

10   9   8   7   6   5   4   3   2   1

To the sketchbook –

that time honored repository of the inane

and the ineffable.

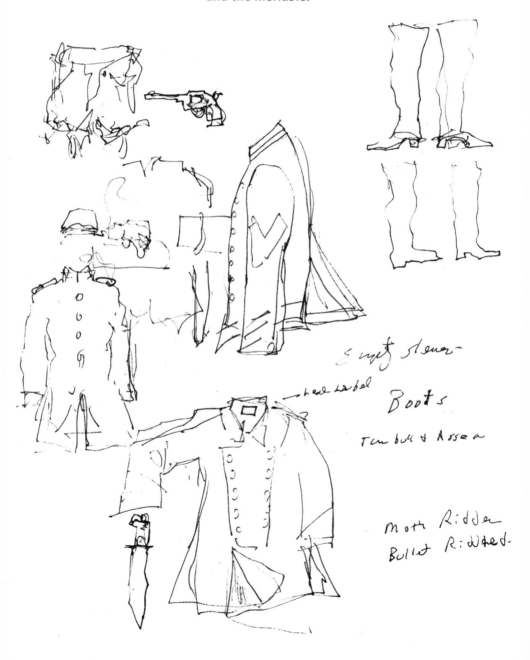

Bad Dog

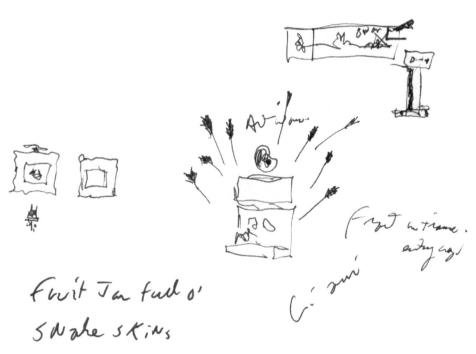

Fruit Jar full o'
Snake skins

Contents

Alluvia—

mississippi

YAZOO   Talahatchie

4'6" 6'6"

2'

MISSISSIPPI

YAZOO

LEFLORE

TALAhatchie.

Leflore

Words and Pictures

ARTISTS KEEP SKETCHBOOKS. Mine, more than four decades' worth, are filled with visual shorthand. There are drawings and ideas for paintings, sculptures, installations—along with phone numbers, grocery lists, things to do, and of course, mindless doodles. I find critiques of my work, sometimes harsh, alongside welcome fragments of dialogue next to drafts and outlines for fiction.

These hybrid sketchbooks/journals have recently, as if of their own volition, come down from a high shelf in my studio to a table within easy reach. From time to time, out of curiosity, I open one. The working drawings are viable, the rants at times amusing, but it's the vein of narrative that rushes up from the page like charged found objects that interests me most.

When asked, I call what I do Hypothetical Realism. The places and things I paint are not real, but they could be. The same holds true for *Short Mean Fiction*. None of what I have written really happened, but it could have.

Like tales from the Old Testament, these stories are mean, rampant with sex, violence, and death. All are figments of an active, if not fertile, imagination and brevity may be their greatest charm. They are fictions through and through, and should a disclaimer be needed, consider it made.

The drawings scattered throughout this volume are not illustrations, but live in the same place—the sketchbooks—where I first wrote the stories, forgot them, then found them again. To my mind, that's what can be trusted.

As with painting, I feel little pride of authorship and make no literary claims for *Short Mean Fiction*.

For what it's worth, for better or worse, and to my utter surprise, there are many more where these came from.

—WILLIAM DUNLAP

SHORT
MEAN
FICTION

models fast to
continuous pictures?   &   St sebastian of the plains

SAINT SEBASTIAN
of
the

4

P L A I N S

BLACK ~ silke Padow

At for Milling

Do something in old handkerchiefs
NOSE Gag.

✩   Frs

A CLEAN AIR ACT

I magine a blisteringly beautiful day with azure-blue sky. Everything in sharp focus. Exhilarating. Invigorating. Life's possibilities seem endless. These words accurately describe the morning of the last day of Westerfield's life.

He rolled over and looked past the forest of tangled dark hair. He had often run his hands through those unkempt locks and had lately pleasured himself in the firm young flesh they crowned, the memory redolent and refreshing.

Now he looked beyond it all to the open window that let some of the rich atmosphere into their upper rooms on the third floor of this Victorian B&B built high over the water on stilts. The two of them had occupied these quarters for most of the summer. It had been transporting but was now coming to an end.

Westerfield was in a complete state of undress when he walked over to the bank of sea-facing windows. The letter containing dried and dead flowers had arrived yesterday and lay crumpled on the floor, its envelope torn to pieces. He pushed it aside with his bare foot, parted the lace curtains, and leaned out into the world, breathing it all in.

Looking to his left and then right, Westerfield stared down at the jagged rocky shoals, which could not be seen at high tide. It was all heart-achingly beautiful. He had never been more at peace.

He sensed a warm, familiar, comforting presence behind him. A hand on his shoulder, the other in the small of his back—firm, knowing, forceful. Westerfield leaned back to receive the embrace.

What he felt was a sharp push, and he was flying out the window, free of all architecture. Westerfield fell and fell and observed in this, his last instant of consciousness as the rocks rushed up to receive him:

If only I had taken rooms on the bayside of the house.

A HIGH SEASON FOR
SELF-INFLICTED WOUNDS

espect the laws of unintended consequences.
Respect the laws of unintended consequences.
Respect the laws . . .
Over and over he wrote on the blackboard as Mrs. Slocum sat at her desk.

Respect the laws of unintended consequences.

One-hundred times.

Lanier turned the words over in his head. Were there such laws?

He loved breaking rules, getting away with small crimes. He'd perfected the art of lying while looking his victim right in the eye. He was, after all, a boy in seventh grade, destined for law school and his father's firm.

Respect the laws of unintended . . .

"Mrs. Slocum? I'm done."

She glanced at the board and saw that Lanier had skipped every number that ended in 7—gone from 6 to 8, 16 to 18, 26 to 28, and so on.

"Young man, give me another fifty, neat and orderly on ruled paper!"

He sat down, opened his desk drawer, and there, wrapped in a handkerchief, was the derringer. It had gone missing from his grandfather's glass case on Easter Sunday. Lanier had picked the lock and stolen the antique gun along with a handful of .22-caliber cartridges.

He unwrapped the silver-plated, pearl-handled piece no bigger than his hand and slipped two rounds into the chamber.

Mrs. Slocum's auburn hair was drawn up in a bun. Her pronounced widow's peak pointed straight down toward her aquiline nose, which led Lanier's eye to her gently heaving breasts, which found a resting place on the edge of her desk. She didn't look up but continued to read from a stack of dismal essays on evolution turned in by Lanier's classmates.

He'd always liked Mrs. Slocum. When she said his name, "Lay-neah," a smile played at the edge of her mouth. He imagined her getting dressed in the morning, putting her hair up, powdering her body as he'd seen his mother do countless times before she died.

Now he stood in front of Mrs. Slocum, derringer in hand, double-action hammer cocked. The part in her hair pointed straight as a plumb line down to her nose, between those breasts to her navel and whatever else lay in the path of his imagination or a small-caliber bullet.

Coming back from lunch today, Lanier had positioned a sun-dried and flattened feline carcass on top of the doorjamb so that the first person entering would experience the dubious pleasure of a petrified cat striking them on the head. The smell was almost gone; its face, fur, and collar were intact.

That first person was not Mrs. Slocum, as Lanier had hoped, but Felicity Farber, who screamed, wet her pants, and called the cat by name.

Parents, nurses, even a police car came. After all the fuss, it was just Lanier and Mrs. Slocum alone, staying after school until their respective tasks were completed.

"Mrs. Slocum?"

"Are you sure you're through this time, Lay-neah?"

"Yes, ma'am."

She looked up and saw Lanier with the pistol raised. The smile that lived at the corners of her mouth froze in place.

Both barrels fired simultaneously. The derringer's report made a peculiar, high-pitched, spitting sound. The only other noise was the shattering of a single pane of glass in the window that looked out over the playground.

That's where Lanier would have been after a normal school day, horsing around with his friends, throwing knives, exchanging cigarettes and those wallet-sized booklets that portrayed familiar cartoon characters engaged in the most egregious sex acts imaginable.

Everyone on the playground stopped and looked up at the window. It had been smashed by the .22-caliber projectiles an instant after they'd passed through the ill-formed, immature, adolescent brain of Sidney Lanier Wannamaker III.

A LIFE WELL LIVED

Wonderful," "marvelous," "stupendous," "spectacular" were not just often-used superlatives in Lester Weatherly's vocabulary but dramatic, emphatic pronouncements made on all things observed, from phenomena in the natural world to a well-turned ankle or phrase. He'd been known to declare "sublime" the annual May blooming of his penthouse-garden irises, and with martini in hand pull up a chair to watch and record in his botanical journal the progression of each budding flower, from bloom to fade.

He risked being run down on Park Avenue the time he dropped to all fours, mesmerized by an army of ants dismantling and transporting the corpse of a wasp back to their colony on the median. "Extraordinary," he intoned to passersby stepping over him and occasionally onto these highly motivated, organized female worker ants no less intent on success than the ordinary Manhattanite.

Here was a man who, in the parlance of the day, lived in the moment. He relished and was deeply affected by the academic and actual alike. While studying the classics at Cambridge, he had become a favorite of the vicar and Kings College historian John Saltmarsh when the student apprenticed himself to the Master of Grounds, an unlettered, functional illiterate who nonetheless was one with the soil and perfectly embodied the English obsession with gardening.

There were extensive travels in the Orient, as it was then called: the Russian Steppes, Manchuria, Southeast Asia, and the Indian subcontinent. King Sihanouk of Cambodia personally escorted Lester through the ruins of Angkor Wat's temple complex before he traveled on to Ceylon and Siam—ultimately renamed Sri Lanka and Thailand—where he became a scholar of Khmer culture and Buddhist mythology.

His senior position at a grand Wall Street firm gave him ample opportunity to exercise his formidable social skills, acquired during a privileged upbringing among Charleston's Tidewater elite and honed at Sewanee's Kappa Alpha house.

Lester relished the high life and the low, and was a devotee of the downtown New York scene. He hung out with Robert Mapplethorpe and his lover Sam Wagstaff, and can be seen in several Patti Smith photographs documenting life on the Bowery and at the seminal punk-rock venue CBGB's.

He was not entirely trusted by this crowd, given his

background and the fact that he was an unapologetic hyper-heterosexual. Lester had a child with the South African model Swalia Embrace and, by all accounts, was a doting father until the little girl began to talk and he realized she had nothing to say.

Lester Weatherly had encyclopedic knowledge and an elegantly furnished mind. His worldview and empathy were boundless, if at times enigmatic. So it came as a complete surprise to his coterie of friends when, at a dinner party one evening, Lester started to weep. Unnoticed at first, it began with a single tear down his cheek, which was shortly followed by another, accompanied by soft sobs, and ultimately erupted into uncontrollable wailing.

He was inconsolable and escorted to his car by sympathetic, if bewildered, dinner partners. Lester was still blubbering when his driver delivered him to his butler, who helped him into bed. When his tears did not subside, the following morning his personal physician had him admitted to Lenox Hill Hospital. Friends, flowers, and well-wishers arrived, as did a minister, his personal trainer and life coach, even a rabbi to offer opinions and proffer solutions, but all was for naught.

It is something of an irony that the chemical makeup of human tears and saline solution is, for all intents and purposes, the same. The latter was introduced intravenously into Lester and kept him alive, but not for long. He willfully wasted away without taking nourishment or uttering a single syllable.

Wild speculation followed the news of Lester's mysterious demise and was the talk of *haute* New York for day and days. Toward the end, his only sister, Chastain, had come up from Nashville to be with him and tend to his affairs. When cleaning out his hospital room she found there, under his pillow, a dog-eared, tear-stained, paperback copy of Eric Siegel's novella, *Love Story*.

She dared not tell a soul.

A FABLE OF THE HOLY SEE

History's first one-armed Pope had, through antics and edicts, earned the moniker Pious the Unpleasant.

As an adolescent the future Pope lost his arm in a masturbation accident, not an uncommon occurrence for young men caught up in his generation's obsession with Onanism. God's grace is munificent, and the future Pope rose in the ranks of the church by publicly beating his breast with his remaining fist and loudly decrying his sin.

Often with trauma, other appendages will rise to the occasion, and their strengths can multiply to compensate for the missing limb. In The Unpleasant's case, it was his penis that answered the call and acquired a dexterity and reach that was, to coin a phrase, the envy of all Christendom.

The Holy Unit developed a persona separate and in some ways superior to Pious. With the aid of a specially adapted stylus, it could write Latin encyclicals in a voice all its own. Its wisdom and cunning were legend, and few dared debate, disparage, or disappoint it. All would bow down before this Pope and his infallible phallus.

Now Protestants were in full revolt in Gaul, and Ottoman warships were in the Bosphorus Straits, closing in on Constantinople. The Pope and his empowered penis were put to the ultimate test: how to hold heretics and infidels at bay while satisfying the needs of clergy. As in ancient days, when bread and circuses were ubiquitous as barbarians stormed the gates of Rome, altar boys seemed to provide the obvious solution.

A festival would be celebrated simultaneously across the land. Decreed by a Papal Bull, duly ordained and named for Saint Pedophilia, it was to be christened "The Sacred Running of the Altar Boys." Not only would this give relief to the exhausted male bovines who had been mercilessly pursued since pagan times, it would aid and abet the recruitment of young friars while formally recognizing sodomy, a practice rampant in the Church and only occasionally interrupted by the impediment of full-length liturgical vestments.

This solution would be short-lived, for it did not take Constantinople long to be renamed Istanbul or for numerous cathedrals to become mosques. European bloodlines grew scarce and diluted. Blonde hair and blue eyes darkened with each passing generation. Apparently, praying five times a day did not preclude conjugal visits to the women's side of worship houses.

The prodigious Papal Penis began to write less and less; it withered and went for days without arousal. Erectile dysfunction was yet to enter the medical lexicon, nevertheless this malady was reported far and wide, from the private apartments of Cardinals in Castel Sant'Angelo to the humble abodes of lowly parish priests. The lethargy was universal—in a word, Catholic.

Altar boys were to disappear along with the Latin Mass, yet young men still found themselves vulnerable to their military superiors, tribal leaders, pedagogues, imams, and self-proclaimed holy men. They would grow up in turn to participate in the tradition of sexual exploitation of the weak and take their proper place in the religious and civic orders of the day.

As for the once-magisterial Papal Penis, in Rome, somewhere deep in the bowels of St. Peter's Cathedral, amongst the stores of outdated and antiquated relics, inside an oil-filled ampoule adorned with rubies, emeralds, and gold filigree, remains the shrunken, shriveled, ink-stained foreskin of Pious the Unpleasant, who is remembered, if at all, as history's only one-armed Pope.

OPEN ALL NIGHT

The hungry customers who filled the place were a cross-section of gender, age, class, and race. It was late of a Saturday night, soon to be Sunday morning, and all fell silent and statue-still when the exchange got loud, its intensity apparent.

"Honey, you'd sooner get a certified letter from Satan as to mess with me tonight" was a direct quote from the waitress to a disheveled old boy standing there looking all roughed-up and used.

The only sounds audible were bacon frying and coffee brewing, and their respective smells were having a Pavlovian effect on the Waffle House crowd. The young man in question was unshaven and wearing a vintage, which is to say dirty, yellow Caterpillar hat cocked to one side. A misbuttoned plaid shirt partially tucked into his new Levi's with tags still attached, muddy boots, and an over-sized silver bull-riding rodeo belt buckle rounded out his ensemble.

Our waitress stood square-shouldered with feet planted in her hard-earned and rightful place behind the Waffle House counter. They both stared long and hard at one another. One of the patrons—the one with her cell phone out—took note of the wooden plates on the handle of a .38-caliber snub-nose Smith & Wesson revolver protruding from the old boy's right back pocket, where the red bandanna should have been. His hands were on his hips just inches from the aptly named "Saturday-night special." He brought his palms up slowly and held them out flat, as if pushing against an invisible wall.

"I do not want no trouble," he said emphatically. "Just my bacon-and-egg sandwich."

The waitress had been holding a paper bag the whole time, which she threw and he caught. Their eyes remained locked.

Sizzle, sizzle—

Drip, drip—

"Tomatoes?" he asked.

"On the side" was her detached and even reply. "This one's on the house," she said.

"Don't want no trouble."

"You go home and see to them children," she implored.

"Yes, ma'am," were his last words as he eased out and into the dark.

Outside, the door of a pickup truck opened and shut, an aging engine cranked, and gears ground into reverse. Headlights came on and washed the parked cars with brilliant white light. A collective sigh of relief was audible in the small, tightly packed space. The waitress opened the cash register and, from her apron pocket, deposited several bills and some change.

"That's my boy," she said to no one in particular as she gently closed the register. "He ain't been out long and don't rightly know how to talk to folks."

The parking lot came alive with flashing blue lights and the sound of a siren. Tires squealed, men shouted and cursed, and the Waffle House clientele rushed to the windows, cell phones on photo and video mode.

Then came the sound of a .38-caliber pistol. A very loud *POW!* followed by the staccato report of 9-millimeter Glocks: *Pop, pop, pop. Pop. Pop-pop.* Patrons screamed and hit the floor; some crawled under tables.

The waitress had not moved. She stood behind the counter, holding onto the cash register for physical if not moral support. As if on command from a higher power, the register slowly opened. She stared down at the neatly ordered drawer with its divisions for bills—twenties, tens, fives, ones—and compartments for quarters, dimes, nickels, pennies. Here was universal order, a place for everything and everything in its place.

The waitress took a great deal of comfort in that.

DR. KEY LLOYD:
ADVENTURES IN MEDICINE

Of all the leisons Dr. Lloyd had seen or read about, hers was his favorite. Slightly raised, pink, blue, and on occasion bright-red, it was a full four inches long and ran diagonally across her rib cage under her right arm, ending very near her breast. Given that hospital gowns open in the back he was, during her convalescence, to become quite familiar with that particular place on her body.

She claimed the scar was numb, yet when, under the guise of examination, Dr. Lloyd fondled or kissed it, she shuddered as though he had stimulated her clitoris or nipple. She would never tell him how she got the scar, so, to her utter delight, night after night he invented tales of the scar's provenance and told her the stories in a quiet but fervent whisper.

One fabricated account had her side pierced by white-hot shrapnel during a Vietcong mortar attack in the Mekong Delta circa 1968. (She had not yet been born.) Then there was the I-75 rollover accident when her black SUV ended upside down in the Everglades amongst a gaggle of rutting alligators. Another elaborate narrative attributed the scar to her narrowly escaping the ire of New England Puritans during the Salem witch hysteria.

So angry a scar could have been made by hooded captors wielding hot pokers during the Spanish Inquisition, in which her answer to any question would have been wrong and potentially fatal. There were bullfighting scenarios, as well as a gold-filled galleon pillaged by Blackbeard and his lusty crew. There she was at the Romanov executions, and on board an observation balloon fired upon during the Battle of the Somme.

(Feel free to insert your own here.)

There were a thousand-and-one possibilities, but the truth was far less dramatic, if no less romantic. She had become entangled in a Tallahatchie County barbed-wire fence after an assignation in a duck blind with her husband's best friend. Birds were flying everywhere, but the only shot fired had been down her throat, and she couldn't tell Dr. Lloyd that.

(Aside: the marriage did not survive.)

She was, in fact, beginning to embrace, even believe, these alternative explanations and could not wait for Dr. Lloyd to make his rounds, initiate an examination, and relate the next installment. The scar got no rest and took on a life of its own, becoming anxious, irritated, and yet was an integral part of their foreplay and the only real thing they had in common.

Late one night, when Dr. Lloyd touched his tongue to the sensitive area, he felt something sharp. With his teeth he drew out a small shard of metal—bright and shiny as stainless steel. He showed her the splinter, and when she held out her hand, it pricked her. Cool, clear, spring-like liquid streamed from the wound. The scar began to fade, disappear, as did her other symptoms: chronic nausea, chills, fevers, emotional outbursts, screams, and the cursing of God and His angels.

All that was left was a single drop of blood pooling in her palm.

GAINFUL EMPLOYMENT

The drugstore opened at 8 a.m. sharp, and Laurie was always there, prompt and eager as in all things. Her first year of college was behind her, and she was on her own with a summer job. Laurie's father was still away, her mother was going through the change and, since being laid off at the munitions plant, was a holy terror. It was good to be away from all of that.

At the drugstore her tasks included stocking merchandise, making milkshakes and Coke floats, and selling war-surplus condoms that the druggist, Mr. Lunsford, acquired by the gross. Laurie was never embarrassed by these prophylactic transactions, though many of her patrons were. She generally purloined a few rubbers each day, which was a good thing given that she and Bryce, another boarder at Mrs McClure's Greek Revival manse-turned-boarding-house, had begun a torrid and only somewhat clandestine affair. Pregnant was the last thing Laurie wanted to be.

Bryce's part-time job at the hardware store gave him time off to play semi-pro baseball. Sometimes he was gone for days, and Laurie pined for him pitifully until Walter,

Bryce's best friend from high school, mustered out of the Navy and came home to exercise his G.I. Bill at the local college. He took the room next to Bryce.

Walter was charming, mature, and worldly. He had circumnavigated the globe and been stationed in the Philippines. Laurie and Bryce were inseparable, and Walter eased effortlessly into the role of intimate friend and confidant to both. At times of an evening he would watch them make love and masturbate.

When Bryce boarded the bus with the baseball team for a five-day, nine-game series, he asked Walter to look after Laurie, knowing exactly what would happen—and it did that very night.

At nineteen and in the bloom of her youth, Laurie was tall, poised, and handsome, with colt-like movements. She was sensual and ripe. All those dire warnings and Sunday-school drivel about hellfire and brimstone notwithstanding, she and her body knew it was their time.

The *menage a trois* began when Bryce got back from his road trip. The team had won only two games. He had struck out repeatedly, committed numerous errors, and collided hard with an outfielder chasing a lazy pop-up fly. Bryce was beat-up, sore, and humiliated.

Back at Mrs. McClure's boardinghouse, he confided to Walter and Laurie that he was considering hanging it all up. Laurie began to massage his sore shoulder; a bottle of

bourbon came out, candles were lit, and clothes came off. Before she knew it, Laurie was on the bed servicing Bryce orally with Walter behind her pushing deeper and deeper until all three climaxed more or less at the same time.

This was a revelation for the three young adults, and variations on their new arrangement were repeated nightly. There was still the occasional one-on-one encounter when either Walter or Bryce could get Laurie alone, but for the most part they generally fell asleep together, spent and exhausted, with early wake-up calls in the morning.

Laurie had never felt so pampered, so needed. The boys couldn't do enough for her. They said the sweetest things and included her in every conversation. Walter and Laurie went to see Bryce play in his last Saturday-night home game. He got three hits, drove in a run, and made sensational defensive plays from his position at third base.

All were exuberant and a little tipsy when they got home from the post-game celebration. Walter had jerry-rigged, with waterproof cloth and tape, a steam room in their communal tile bath. They stripped down and entered the warm, wet, exotic environment. Body parts were caressed and rubbed. Laurie was the center of attention and soon found herself covered from head to toe with mineral oil. Bryce led Laurie to the bed and, placing a pillow under her, began to kiss and enter her the old-fashioned way. She lost track of Walter's whereabouts and was only roused from her reverie when Bryce seemed to flinch, as if interrupted. She adjusted to his quickened motion as he rose up and groaned.

Laurie glanced at the wall, where shadows from the flickering candle revealed two figures in profile, one snugged up tight behind the other. Laurie looked up at Bryce, his face contorted in pain or ecstasy—she could not tell which. Two hands grasped his waist from behind, reached out to his chest, and found his nipples. She felt Bryce rigid within her and from his lips came "Oh, my God."

Apparently all those rumors were true.

"Goddamn Navy," Laurie thought, but not out loud.

Bryce and Walter were still locked in the arms of Morpheus as Laurie gently extracted herself from the threesome. She quietly made her way to her own room, packed all her belongings in two suitcases, and began the mile-and-a-quarter walk to the campus of Broadwater Baptist College for Women.

The sun was just coming up on this third Sunday in August 1946 when Laurie appeared at the steps of Little John Lattimore Residence Hall. The dorm mother, Miss Hortense Montague, was sitting alone on the stoop, a cup of coffee in one hand, cigarette in the other, and a Bible on her lap. She looked up and broke into a broad smile when she recognized the young woman, suitcases in hand.

"May I come in?" Laurie asked meekly.

"Why, yes indeed, my dear child. School doesn't start

until next week, don't you know, but there's always room for our star English major and budding poet."

Laurie shuffled a bit, then started up the stairs.

"My, my, but you look bushed. Have you come a long way? Did you have a nice summer?"

THE FIELD

He had clear and pristine memories of being told of the battle—a skirmish, really—on his grandfather's Virginia farm in the summer of 1863.

A Confederate battery, some infantry. and a smattering of unattached cavalry, six of whom are buried here, were bivouacked on the property, out from but in sight of the big house. His great-grandfather Luke, and Ash, the old Negro manservant who had stayed and been assigned to the boy, watched from the upstairs gallery as a column of Union soldiers marched unannounced across the Rebel front.

The ground was flat and unencumbered by forest, much as it is today: ideal for grazing livestock, military maneuvers, or three-acre lots for casual country living.

The Rebels scurried about, whooping and hollering, and unlimbered their single smoothbore, nine-pounder Napoleon brass cannon. The cavalry saddled up and mounted with enthusiasm as the surprised and confused Union recruits, who had been in Washington City two days earlier, broke ranks and milled about.

The Union officers had managed to lose the ridge road that would have taken them safely into Winchester and, by misreading a compass heading, had ended up on the more or less deserted Coleman farm, whose young men were either entrenched around Richmond or dead. The Coleman slaves had turned contraband, except for old Ash, who had stayed behind out of curiosity or lethargy or both.

He had first heard these stories during a childhood of summers spent with his maternal grandparents on this farm while his mother gallivanted around the country spending alimony money in search of a mythical fountain of youthful men.

The Rebel cavalry were a motley lot, no more than two dozen from Mississippi, Alabama, and Texas whose units had been badly used at Brandy Station. They did not lack for spunk or élan, having acquired captured horses, boots, and Henry repeating rifles. Mounted at last, they cantered off to the right in high demonstration, hoping to cut off any retreat by the Union detachment now marching back-and-forth to contradictory orders before eventually forming some sort of line to receive the inevitable and honor-bound charge.

Late into his eighties, his grandfather would walk the fields after a heavy rain looking for belt buckles, pieces of tack,

Minie balls, and the like. He was seldom disappointed. One of the great mysteries of these archaeological ventures was the occasional arrowhead or pottery shard that rose to the surface, suggesting that the skirmish of 1863 was not the first conflict these fields had witnessed.

The Rebel battery fired three rounds of solid shot that landed harmlessly behind the Union troops. Next they loaded canister, the artillery's equivalent of buckshot, and waited. The dismounted cavalry began firing down the Union line, causing much consternation. Then, as if by Providence, a Union caisson, pulled by a span of mules and hauling a spanking new 12-pounder Whitworth rifled breech-loading gun, came up on their rear. The Rebels overwhelmed the Federal teamsters, mounted their mules, and rode the Yankee trophy back to their position amid much laughter, hat throwing, and huzzahs. None of them knew how to operate the English-made Whitworth, but that did not stop the boys in butternut from loading—overloading, really—and firing in the general direction of the bright-blue line. It was not yet 9 a.m. on this June morning. Confederate coffee was boiling on campfires; the smell of side-meat frying filled the air.

He inherited the farm and its fields after his grandfather's death. There had been offers from real-estate developers to subdivide and gate into community this much fought-over field whose ground would not stop belching up evidence: cups, forks, a rusty Navy Colt cap-and-ball pistol with four chambers undischarged; and even an old tintype bearing the faded image of a young woman. And then there was the occasional piece of bone, either man or mule: artifacts all from a piece of ground that could and often did speak.

The skirmish went on all day, one side prevailing and then the other. Southern troops marching to the sound of gunfire reinforced the ragtag Rebels and doubled their numbers by late morning. Repelled in their first assaults, they were preparing for another when the Confederate ad hoc gun crew managed to ignite the black powder charges in the captured caisson and blow themselves and the Whitworth gun to bits—killing mules, horses, men, and igniting a fire that covered the field in smoke. Visibility and breathing became nigh unto impossible.

The family's oral history was sustained by the inspired and lyrical accounts of "The Battle of Coleman's Farm" by one Rufus Jennings, a young poet from Bristol, Virginia, who survived the war, as did his journal. The official Union report was written by Levi Farnsworth, the company's historian from Brockton, Massachusetts, whose dry, measured, but accurate entries are nonetheless invaluable for the mind's reconstruction of the day. According to both Jennings and Farnsworth, a hard rain came in early afternoon, soaking everything and everyone. Nature provided a welcome respite, and the water collected filled canteens and cooled heated brows.

When the rain let up, a dense fog joined with the oily smoke as both Union and Confederates formed ranks for what all hoped would be a final assault. Officers barked orders, a bugler sounded the charge, a drummer beat a staccato tattoo. With bayonets fixed, both sides marched double-quick into glory or oblivion. The field was engulfed in an abnormal, earthbound cloud that hovered like a sandstorm from hell, obscuring everything that entered it. The clash of men and horses, metal and wood, made for sounds horrifying and unique. Curses, moans, yells, and pleas, God's name invoked in vain and praise, all uttered and emitted from the cloud as sightless men, without strategy or tactics, went at one another like two armed mobs. Every now and again something would be ejected from the maelstrom: a man running or crawling, looking over his shoulder; two men, one in blue, the other gray, helping each other with no obligation to cause or nation save their mutual humanity. The fog lifted. The smoke began to clear.

The chroniclers, as if writing in unison, noted the sudden appearance of a double rainbow. Some men dropped their weapons, as if divine intervention had brought an end to the fray. All was quiet now except for the occasional cry from a wounded or dying soldier.

Thirst and fear are universal attributes of battle. The

old Negro and the boy filled water buckets from the house well and walked into the field. They could administer to the thirst but only observe the fear.

The soon-to-be-freed Ashland Cornelius Coleman was born in the late 18th century and had never ventured far from the Coleman farm. Nonetheless, he had seen and knew much. According to family legend, Ash walked amongst the quick and the dead, speaking to those who could hear him and those who could not.

"White folks, y'all got to stop this mess," said Ash, with as much disgust as dismay.

He shook the motionless shoulder of a corpse.

"Quit this foolishness," he commanded, kicking the booted foot of another.

"You'uns come to yo' senses now!"

He offered water to lips barely alive.

"White folks, y'all is crazy."

HIGH SCHOOL FOOTBALL

Fran Flowers was a junior, long-limbed and athletic. She stood a full head taller than the other cheerleaders and had an engaging way of rolling her eyes as if to ask, "Will this high school BS ever be over?"

A senior, Galt McDermott was taller still and seemed to grow some every day. He was a starter on defense for the Blue Springs Bearcats and backed up the quicker and more elusive Keyshawn Wardlow at wide receiver.

Last spring, Fran traveled with the Bearcat track team to the tri-state meet. When her roommate, Renata, the shot putter, fell ill, Fran found herself alone in a Birmingham hotel room with Coach Ambrose, who proposed to personally treat her strained hamstring. A little analgesic balm on the inner thigh led to clitoral stimulation followed by an arduous night of physical engagement and sexual exploration. This led to weekly sessions with Coach Ambrose in his office, the back of his van, and once in a Sunday-school room where Fran was introduced to, among other procedures, the peculiar opportunities and obligations of anal intercourse.

Coach Ambrose resigned abruptly to take a position as director of a Presbyterian boys camp in Tyler, Texas, where he now awaited arraignment on four counts of child molestation. His heterosexual proclivities never came to light, but Fran and several girls at Blue Springs High exchanged knowing glances when they passed in the hall.

Fran told Galt all of this soon after they started seeing one another. Not out of guilt or shame but to let him know it was an option were he interested, which of course he was. A sore ass was lot better than coming up pregnant, Fran reasoned.

Keyshawn Wardlow had a fever of 101 degrees when he dressed out for the Coldwater game. The Copperheads were up two scores on the Bearcats in the fourth quarter when Keyshawn went down and didn't get up. Coaches and trainers came out, and finally an ambulance took him away.

"McDermott, get in there for Wardlow," Coach Hardy grunted.

Forty-four fake left—tinderbox on two, a classic hook-and-go, would be Galt's first offensive play of the season. Keyshawn hadn't done a great deal, and the Coldwater defense didn't expect much from his substitute. But the Blue Springs sophomore quarterback, Brent Frohm, and Galt had grown up together, were in fact cousins who'd spent countless hours playing catch, and intuitively knew each other's tendencies.

When the ball was snapped, Galt fired out of his three-point stance and sold the inside-hook fake to the DB, who came up fast. Brent's pump-fake was perfect. Galt planted his left foot, pivoted 360 degrees, and was at full speed when Brent lofted the ball into his outstretched hands. Forty-five yards later he crossed the goal line. Extra point, good.

Galt ran back to a Blue Springs bench gone berserk. To the surprise of no one, an onside kick was called. Galt took his position to the right of the kicker. The Copperheads were all up on the line in anticipation of the short kick. The ball arced up and sailed well beyond the mandatory ten yards. Galt sprinted through the line, went high in full stride, caught the live ball, and glided into the end zone untouched. Extra point, good. Score tied.

Fans were out of their seats. Players, coaches, and cheerleaders mingled about, hooting and hollering and jumping up-and-down. Galt brushed by Fran as he jogged back to the sidelines, caught her scent, and tried to catch her eye.

"Get your mind on the ballgame, McDermott," intoned the ever-observant Coach Hardy.

Galt sat out the kickoff and went in at strong safety. On third-and-eight the Coldwater QB threw a pass that was tipped. Galt gathered it in and returned to the twelve yard-line before being run out of bounds. Three running plays got the ball to the four. With six seconds left, the ever-shaky kicker was asked to make the equivalent of an extra point for the win. Brent bobbled a bad snap, defensive linemen converged, and overtime seemed imminent. Brent threw the ball where he knew only Galt would be—deep in the left corner of the end zone, alone.

With three TDs and one interception in less than six minutes, Galt McDermott's reputation in the small town of Blue Springs was secure, at least until next week, when the Bearcats would play the 8-and-0 Pulaski Academy Patriots.

Adolescent boys never go anywhere alone when they can go in a pack. After celebration and showers, two carloads headed toward the Blue Springs Hospital at a high rate of speed to check on Keyshawn. Among them were Fran, Purvis "Parson" Weems, and Rick "Ricardo" Rawls, the 4'10" bandy-legged savant Galt and company kept around for amusement. Ricardo knew and could sing every song recorded since World War II, recite and act-out most movies. He also proved useful on science and math quizzes.

The nurse at the reception desk eyed the exuberant throng suspiciously. This crowd seemed far too jolly to be in the ER at 11:30 p.m. on a Friday night.

"Help you?" she asked, clearly irritated.

"Want to see about our buddy Keyshawn Wardlow," said "Parson" Weems, answering for all. "Ambulance brought him in about nine."

The nurse picked up a stack of file cards from her desk and leisurely thumbed through them. "What's that name again?"

"Wardlow. Keyshawn Wardlow."

The nurse looked up, held out a card. "You boys done come to the wrong place."

"Say what?"

The nurse chose her words carefully. "Better check the morgue."

"The hell you say!"

"Bullshit!"

"God damn!"

"That can't be!" erupted the Blue Springers.

"Hold it down, hold it down, we got sick here." A red-faced, large-bellied orderly with RON emblazoned on his nametag rushed up. "Y'all go out and come back in like civilized human beings," ordered orderly RON as he grabbed Galt by the arm.

"Get your goddamn hands off me," Galt spat, and jerked away.

At that moment, the Reverend Wilbur Wardlow and his wife came into the ER, looking most concerned. Fran went to head them off as Galt vaulted the reception desk, shouldered the nurse aside, and begin rifling through her file cards.

"Here, here! Now, now!" A new voice from an older man in a white coat cut through the cacophony. Galt recognized Dr. Benjamin Mallard as one of Fran's father's golfing buddies and immediately went up to him, hushing the gathered throng.

"Dr. Mallard?" Galt said. "Keyshawn Wardlow was brought here from the Coldwater game. Is he okay?'"

"Why, yes indeed. Treated him myself. Three liters of saline and some glucose. That boy has the flu in the worst way. Fever was 102.2. Shoulda never been on that field. He's in room 324B. By the way," he said, "as for the Coldwater game, you boys done good. Congratulations!"

RON fumed as he watched this pacifying exchange. Behind the registration desk the nurse read from a file card.

"'Scuse me. I got one Castor Wildeman, black male, 5 feet, 11 inches, 175 pounds, DOA. Possible drug overdose. Sorry if there was any confusion."

After leaving Keyshawn's room, Galt went directly to the nurses' desk, his entourage in tow. "Where's RON?"

"On break. Outside. Waiting on you I expect."

Galt slammed through the ER doors at a full run and found RON with two other orderlies smoking on the loading dock. RON saw them, stepped on his cigarette, and came at Galt with a slow right hand that was easily dodged. Galt's fist sunk into a belly that was the softest thing he'd ever hit—then his left found a kidney. RON turned, and Galt grabbed his collar with one hand, the seat of his pants with the other, and cake-walked him to the railing, slamming his face against the bars and forcing RON down to the concrete.

The two orderlies started to intervene in a half-hearted way. Galt held up his hand, "Don't even think about it.

Sharon = Lib nata   55 ¢ per $495
Deb~ Brooks -   301 - 405 1478
            m t At museum-----

J. Parker -
AP . ¥ 333 4112
S'Ann -
Steve Brown - Jackson School - Photo Show
            669 1965   592·0675   Maria James

When asked, and you will be asked, you will say RON swung first."

"Yes, sir."

"Sure enough."

"Easy now."

RON crawled onto all fours. His outsized butt presented an irresistible target, and a quick kick to the testicles brought events to a proper end.

Galt pulled Fran aside and asked if she would discretely inform her father of this unpleasantness. "I might need some legal advice or maybe even representation."

On their way back to town, Ricky "Ricardo" Rawls was beside himself, re-creating with commentary and sound effects all the evening's activities, to the delight of everyone except Fran.

"Take me home," she demanded under her breath.

Galt shuffled a bit as he walked Fran to the door of the Flowers' three-story brick Georgian home. He apologized for the fight and his friends. This was not how they had hoped the evening would progress.

Fran turned abruptly and said, "Here's what you'll do: dump those idiot friends of yours, come back, park down the street. The back gate and poolhouse will be open. I'll talk to Dad, then meet you. Be very, very quiet."

Fran's father, Judge Winston Flowers, found the events of the evening rather amusing and agreed to help Galt if need be. She kissed him goodnight, spent a little time in the bathroom, and made a big show of closing her bedroom door before slipping down the back stairs. A full moon illuminated the town of Blue Springs in a warm, embracing light, casting rich, dark shadows. Fran slowly opened the French doors of the poolhouse. In it was a double bed, bathroom, and kitchenette. Along the back wall, louvered doors opened to a walk-in closet.

Fran whispered: "Galt, you here?"

"You bet!" was the reply.

"Are you alone?"

"Of course."

"Shhhhhh!!!"

Fran and Galt's consensual acts of coitus were perfunctory and efficient. They undressed each other and stood entwined. Hands, lips, and tongues worked to stimulate every pleasure center. Moans, breathless groans, and invocations of various deities were emitted. Then came alternating sessions of fellatio and cunnilingus.

Fran readily admitted to being something of a screamer; a rolled washcloth was often between her teeth. They worked their way through a myriad of positions: missionary, dog-fashion, double-blind overlap, him on top, and so forth until she maneuvered Galt onto his back, straddled him, and began the slow, rolling motions that would inevitably lead to elevated levels of sensuality and nonverbal communication for them both.

It worked every time. The difference tonight was that this pageant of lust and flesh, usually performed in the dark, was played out in the light of a full Harvest Moon. It was a stunning and erotic visual spectacle.

Fran, as per Coach Ambrose's precise instructions, always gave herself a rectal douche followed by a generous application of Preparation H, which not only eased the initial discomfort of anal penetration but helped lubricate as well. Fran had admonished Galt time and again not to deposit a single drop of his manly essence into her vagina. As he came close to completion, Fran lifted herself and reinserted Galt into her anus, which hurt at first but soon gave her an overwhelming sense of mastery and control, to say nothing of a peculiar pleasure that was so far unmatched by any other physical experience in her young life.

They lay there spent in pools of light, perspiration, and over-the-counter lubricants.

"Don't you go to sleep on me," Fran whispered as Galt breathed deeply.

She extracted herself. With a wet cloth she washed her long lean body before doing the same for Galt.

"If my daddy catches you here in the morning, there'll be hell to pay."

"Okay, I'm up. I'm off. I'll lock the gate."

They dressed and straightened the room, touching and caressing each other in the bright, natural illumination.

"Goodnight," Fran said in a manner more declarative than salutary.

"Yes, it was, wasn't it?" Galt sounded almost philosophical.

Then she was gone, dancing from one shadow to the next through the side door, up the stairs, and into her room. She went to the window and smiled as she watched Galt's athletic form move slowly and confidently along the fence. Then he paused, looked back, and held a finger to his lips as if to quiet someone.

The jerking, hand-flinging figure of Ricky "Ricardo" Rawls emerged from the poolhouse door. Fran watched them move together as one, Galt's arm around Ricky's shoulder, into the light and out of sight, laughing.

She stood at the window for a long time before closing the blinds. Her room dark, she slipped into bed. Phenylephrine HCI, the active numbing ingredient in Preparation H, began to fade, as did her anger and rage until Fran was left in the dark with a single, over-arching emotion she would come to know time and again in her encounters with men: a deep and abiding disappointment.

WHAM! BAM! POW!

The prisoners of war were organized into groups of twenty and marched down the towpath to the loading dock to be processed, deloused, and transferred to Rotterdam in new military trucks, then loaded onto the same Liberty ships that had brought the trucks and ferried back across the Atlantic. Upon arrival in the U.S., they would be dispersed into small POW camps across the country, many of them in the American South. Rumors were rampant and scuttlebutt was king, but one thing was certain: the war was over for these men.

Diederik looked the part of a Wehrmacht soldier—tall, blond, blue-eyed, with square jaw and erect posture—but he was in fact a Dutch conscript who despised the Germans. In the spring of 1940, they had washed over the Netherlands like the Zuiderzee at flood stage. The Germans had their way with the entire Dutch population: women, children, and young men were the primary targets of shame, humiliation, and abuse, to say nothing of gypsies, Jews, and Seventh-Day Adventists.

According to Diederik's family lore, crowned heads of

Europe had for centuries forced young men to serve as cannon fodder in their endless religious wars and hapless colonial enterprises.

One of Diederik's comrades, now dead, had received a letter from a cousin captured in North Africa who said he often took the city bus from his internment camp to the R. J. Reynolds Tobacco factory in a place called Winston-Salem and would smoke all the cigarettes he could steal. Obviously, life as a POW wasn't all bad.

The trucks were nowhere to be seen, and Diederik's group of POWs was ordered to sit. The two American guards, bored and distracted, had their Garand M1 rifles slung casually over their shoulders. They wandered off in animated conversation looking for shade.

April's sun warmed the winter soil. Spring promised to be glorious with flowering trees, tulips, and daffodils just beginning to stir. The POWs become restless in the heat. One of their number began to whisper to the others.

"There's no one watching. We must make an escape. If we wade the canal we can disperse into the streets. We do it now! For *der Führer*—for the Fatherland!"

This man was a Prussian officer who had changed into a private's uniform before capture. He was a much feared and despised true-believer who three days before had shot a 16-year-old Estonian conscript for leaving his post. This man was Waffen SS.

No one moved.

"Cowards—all of you! Cowards! If we go now some will get away."

American and British soldiers occupied the entire sector, and anyone trying to escape was sure to be shot. Besides, Diederik and his comrades had just had their first hot meal in weeks. Their future as prisoners of the Americans seemed far more full of promise than had their former status as Hitler's shock troops.

The SS officer kept imploring the men to move. None did except for Diederik. As he rose, the officer smiled and got to his feet.

"One man—one man is with me."

In his right hand, Diederik held a stone as large as an Idaho potato. He looked the German in the eye, clicked his heels, and raised his hand as if to salute. He smashed the stone into the German's forehead, dropping him to his knees. Diederik hit him again and again. The prisoners moved in. One by one they began to kick and hit the Nazi with fists, boots, rocks, and spit.

The American guards ambled back from their shady retreat more irritated than concerned, but their M1s were at the ready, bayonets fixed.

"*Achtung*, you motherfuckers—*achtung!*"

The POWs instinctively put their hands behind their

heads. The bruised and bloodied German lay on the tow-path, his left arm in the canal.

"Son of a bitch," said one GI, rolling the officer over with his foot, which put him half in the canal and half out.

He looked at Diederik and made a motion with his head that all interpreted as permission. The SS officer roused a bit and coughed up blood. Diederik shoved him into the canal and held him underwater, his foot on the German's neck, until the incognito officer struggled no more.

The American reached into his breast pocket, brought out a pack of cigarettes, and offered one to Diederik. It was a Lucky Strike. Then, in one smooth motion, he flipped open a Zippo lighter, produced a flame, and held it out. Diederik lit up, inhaled deeply, and passed the cigarette to the POW on his left. Diederik understood little of this except that he had just killed a man, his first of the war.

The trucks pulled up to the loading dock, and prisoners began to climb aboard. When it came Diederik's turn, one of the guards grabbed his shoulder, spun him around, and thrust into his breast pocket a fresh pack of Lucky Strikes. The GI winked at Diederik, then the two Americans walked away, talking and gesturing excitedly about something they called spring training, Dodgers, and Yankees.

This Diederik understood completely.

WHAT'S FOR SUPPER?

Ethereal has perfect teeth, so large, white, and shiny they seem almost oversized for her face, which is beautiful in a youngish sort of way.

Ethereal is Theros's baby sister, and she happened to see Theros and me together once—buck naked, floundering around in their guest room's queen-size waterbed, something we did with considerable regularity that summer.

The sisters' parents, old hippies named Earl and Ethel, both worked. That might sound counterintuitive, but they did, and the sisters, after completing summer school's obligations, were for the balance of the day pretty much left to their own devices.

When I called the Tuesday after she had observed Theros and me, Ethereal answered the door and invited me in. She allowed as how Big Sis was away on a job interview and wouldn›t be home until supper.

"Would you like a glass of lemon-and-mint artificially-flavored iced tea?" she said in that little Ethereal voice of hers.

"You bet," I was quick to answer.

I took a long drink of iced tea, and Ethereal complimented me on the size and quality of the erection she had witnessed the week before. In due course, she was performing the most comprehensive and enthusiastic act of oral sex it's ever been my pleasure to witness or hear about.

She stripped to the waist and let me fondle her hard little ta-tas but said she was afflicted by the curse and wouldn't let me touch her below the navel. Unfinished business there.

• • •

Summers end, of course, and now Ethereal, with half a dozen menus in the crook of her left arm, was standing behind my new bride, twirling her hair and telling her how beautiful she was. She flashed those teeth and asked Monetta, my precious, deeply devoted, and ever-loving wife, all about herself, then looked right through me before explaining the evening's specials.

I could not help but wonder how it might be to enjoy simultaneous sexual congress with the two of them. They obviously liked one another and, hey, I'm a guy! A man can dream, can't he?

Both Ethereal and Monetta threw their heads back and laughed heartily at some off-color *bon mot* or the other. Their seemingly matched sets of teeth were just extraor-

Triple threat

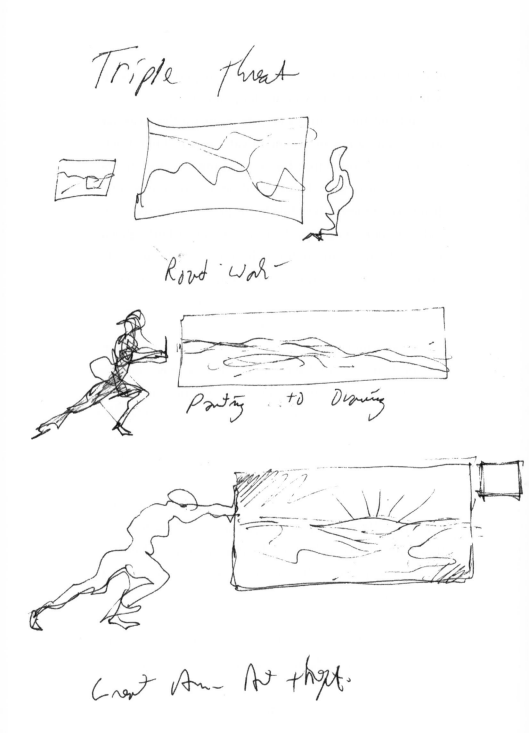

Root Work

Painting to Drawing

Crout Am At thept.

dinary. I couldn't decide which was more perfect, more appealing—or more carnivorous, for that matter.

I ordered the shrimp-and-grits, Monetta the steak tartare—always a raw meat kind of gal. I watched her watching Ethereal, given that I was watching her, too. In the several months since I had called on Theros and become distracted, Ethereal had filled out, grown, matured a bit, and was more gorgeous than ever. Ethereal fairly glided, as though on ice, through the dining room of Silky's, the white-tablecloth, fine-dining restaurant recently opened on Mott Street in downtown Bocograndalusa.

• • •

It is Sunday morning, the sun is shining, roses are blooming and I am surrounded by beauty, both earthly and Ethereal. Monetta has gone to Mobile to visit her dear—and, we hope, soon-to-be departed—mother, whose gallbladder has of late been extracted. Lying with me in our sanctified, consecrated, blissful marital bed are Ethereal and her smushed-faced Pekingese, Loretta.

Now, it's one thing when Ethereal licks my balls, but when I roll her over and mount her in a manly fashion and that damned dog sticks her cold nose up my ass while licking those self-same balls, well, boys, that just ain't right. It ain't natural.

Ethereal just showed up at the front door this morning and asked why I wasn't fishing with Leon (his boat is broke down) and then asked for Monetta. She said the two of them had planned to put on a worship service, it being Sunday and all. Then she asked for a glass of Monetta's sugar-free diet lemonade, which I got for her. And then—well, here we are. Unfinished business, finished.

That damned Loretta turned and snapped at my ankles as she and Ethereal went out the door. Ethereal asked when Leon's boat would be fixed, by Thursday, I say—and when Monetta would be back from Mobile. And would I be out fishing next Sunday?

I asked about the shrimp-and-grits, and if *confit du canard* cassoulet would be on Silky's menu this winter.

She allowed as to how she would look into it. Then she flashed those teeth and smiled, but not with her eyes.

COMPARATIVE RELIGION

Carmelita and Wainwright met in a Virginia Beach hotel at a team-building retreat. It was thought that their professions—public defender and law-enforcement officer, respectively—might benefit from a better understanding one another given the adversarial nature of their jobs and the fact that they would inevitably come in contact with one another during their careers.

Carmelita and Wainwright independently selected full-body-massage sessions over a poetry workshop and a Legos skyscraper competition. They slipped on loose-fitting robes, got paired with one another, and then were led by a saffron-clad Buddhist monk through a myriad of hands-on stretches and awkward positions, including but not limited to leg-behind-head, full-swan improv, slithering snake, handstands, and deep-tissue penetration of various pressure points.

They were delighted to learn from the monk that massage was a central tenet of Theravada Buddhism. Wainwright wryly observed that if the Baptists, his particular denomination of Protestants, ever incorporated full-body massage into the liturgy, they might actually rule the world. A horrifying thought, he concluded.

Carmelita MacGruder's mother was Colombian, her father an Irish engineer. They had met in Cartagena and fallen deeply in love. Carmelita was a devout and practicing Catholic and had been educated, in more ways than one, by Jesuits. They taught her that it was far better to be wrong than ever to be in doubt.

The team-building exercises were to culminate with a midnight fire-walk. Logs were laid out in a 4' x 30' rectangle and set ablaze. The fire was tended for hours and groomed into a bed of banked, glowing-hot coals. At 11:30 p.m. sharp, participants marched to the fire's edge, removed their shoes, and rolled up their pants legs. In a stupor of peer pressure, self-hypnois, and groupthink, they walked swiftly and purposefully across the coals, exiting triumphantly at the far end. It was exhilarating and, for some, a source of immense satisfaction. But not for Carmelita and Wainwright, who opted for an alternative, but equally high-risk, team-building activity.

Their Buddha-sanctioned body-rubbing had proven an irresistible form of foreplay. At 9:00 p.m., when the other team-builders were ensconced in the hotel ballroom watching motivational videos, Wainwright turned up at Carmelita's door with a bottle of Old Weller. The bourbon further stoked their already well-kindled internal flames, whose ferocious heat led them to shed all clothing and inhibitions and pursue their proactive appointment with destiny.

Wainwright stripped and positioned himself behind the buck-naked Carmelita, who had assumed the presentation position on the edge of the bed. She was on her knees, wearing nothing but a tiny gold cross and chain given her by the family priest, who had also instructed her in this submissive posture of worshipful receivership when she was but eleven years old.

Carmelita could not bear to look at Wainwright the Baptist—she buried her face in the hotel pillows and fondled a rosary as she moaned, groaned, recited catechisms and the occasional Hail Mary. The glow from the walkers' fire was reflected in their third-floor window, illuminating the writhing, sweat-drenched bodies.

This went on for quite some time. Carmelita and Wainwright, ever tacit, spoke hardly a word. There was little to say, and there would be time for conversation at breakfast—and, of course, for years to come when they encountered one another in the Halls of Justice.

use cigarette packs

photos of River

wax + screen wire
vaseline + Barbed

Object lesson

sculptured metal +
Palette knife over

area
Photo of
w drawings on

photo   River

M Apr

Photo-
Wax
sculpt int-
Palette kt -
Mail Box -
roll of Barbed wire

Screen wire

shut it up

COMANCHE MOON

Rufus thought it quite remarkable that, there in the moonlight, Sally Erstwhistle looked for all the world like a man, her blonde hair hidden under that wide-brimmed hat, a coarse calico shirt tucked into her dead brother's trousers, the legs stuffed into his boots.

Rufus had insisted that she change out of her plain blue, long-sleeved, neck-to-ankle cotton frock before they mounted the surviving horses and rode out of camp in the dead of night. And she had. Sally had stripped down to what little underclothes she possessed, then pulled garments out of the wagon and the boots off Darden's cold feet.

The war party was likely to come back no matter what, but for a white woman—if they thought her still alive—it was a sure bet. Less so, they figured, for two armed men who had already killed half a dozen of their number.

Rufus had three sisters back in Franklin, Tennessee, and was familiar with women's ways and peculiarities. He had even seen them naked on occasion, but the image of Sally Erstwhistle's lithe form in the heat of the moment stuck with him no matter the arrows flying about and the smell of fear and gunpowder in the air.

"That Sally is bound to make somebody a mighty fine wife," he thought.

The meager caravan they'd started with—three wagons, seven pilgrims, six oxen, a few mules, a milk cow, and several dogs—had camped near a copse of cottonwoods flanking a small, clear stream. They'd planned to stay a day or so to rest the stock before continuing on to Fort Parker and then heading west through what they knew to be Indian country.

They had heard the tales of rape, pillage, fire, and murder, yet some would-be settlers got through unscathed. The Erstwhistle party were law-abiding, God-fearing, praying people. What were the choices? The Lord's will be done.

There was only an hour of sun left when Rufus pointed toward a cloud of dust on the horizon. It grew larger and nearer, and pretty soon the outlines of mounted men riding hard in their direction could be discerned.

Two buffalo hunters, their pack mules loaded with hides and God knows what else, and three Mexican skinners— arrows protruding from the rear ends of the horses and, in some cases, of the men themselves—rode into the camp and quickly dismounted.

"Apaches!" said the red-bearded buffalo hunter as he slipped a Sharps rifle from its sleeve and grabbed a box of 50-caliber cartridges from his saddlebag. They could see the Indians now as well as hear them.

The big, red-bearded man loaded and fired twice at the onrushing horde. One horse and rider went down, and another brave was blown off his pony. All the new arrivals tied their horses, found weapons, and began firing at the fast approaching Indians.

Rufus wasted no time retrieving his lever-action Winchester repeating rifle and government-issue Navy Colt cap-and-ball pistol. Both were loaded, and as the Indian band—no more than a dozen—overrode the camp, Rufus shot one half-naked savage at point-blank range and another as he slid off his pony, a scalping knife in his hand, making for Sally and her long, blonde locks. These were the first men Rufus killed but would not be his last.

As a boy back in Tennessee, he'd lived with and amongst the Cherokee; truth be told, given the cold nights and close quarters, he probably had a little Cherokee in him.

The so-called civilized tribes of the east—the Choctaws, Chickasaws, and Cherokees—were one thing, but Rufus had never seen anything like these horse Indians: small, lean, fearless, and at one with their tough little pinto ponies. They›d strike without warning, kill, torture, rape, and pillage, taking horses, women, and children, all for the hell of it, or so it seemed. They gave no quarter and expected none.

In the few minutes it took the war party to ride through the camp, the warriors killed and scalped two of the Mexicans and Sally's 14-year-old brother, Darden. Mr. Erstwhistle fell to the ground untouched but dead all the same. Sally pulled the pair of old horse pistols from her father's belt and shot one brave in the face and another in the rear end. The red-bearded buffalo hunter found an ax and finished them off.

The Apaches rode back the way they came and regrouped at what they thought a safe distance. The red-bearded buffalo hunter, with his long-range sites and 50-caliber Sharps rifle, dropped two in quick succession. The Indians retreated farther and were soon joined by other warriors shouting insults, jeering, and performing remarkable gymnastics on horseback as they rode contemptuously around the camp shouting threats.

When Rufus signed up in St. Louis, Mr. Erstwhistle had told him he would be responsible for the livestock and would have to pay seven dollars for the pleasure of their company. He could take his meals with the family but must make his bed far away.

"Fair enough," he thought, and then he saw Sally. She was cooking, cleaning, and generally adding an air of domesticity to the rough business of wagon travel. Her mother had died the previous winter; there was about her an air of sadness and resignation, yet her countenance was alluring, beautiful, and aloof.

Now, with her father and brother both gone, Sally was an orphan and alone in the world. Death had most certainly caught up with her, and there was a real question as to whether she and Rufus would survive the night.

The settlers covered their dead with a tarpaulin and tended the wounded as best they could. The four Indian corpses were dragged out of the perimeter a hundred yards or so to bait the Apache warriors into coming in close so they could be shot as well.

Darkness came quickly, and before the moon appeared, six Indians retrieved all their dead, stole the milk cow, and killed the dogs and the red-bearded buffalo hunter, taking his head and his Sharps rifle with them. That was when Rufus decided to set out and asked Sally if she wanted to come along.

So off they rode with an extra horse each roped to their mounts and one of the buffalo hunter's pack mules still loaded with hides and God knows what else. The hunters certainly would not be needing them, being dead and all.

The landscape of undulating hills was pocked with small stands of cottonwood and mesquite. They had to ride below the ridge so as to not be silhouetted by the moon, which ducked in and out from behind summer clouds.

This bright illumination was what dime novelists and historians would come to call a Comanche Moon. In the

4

The eye insert →

maggie

cut canvas   impasto

Colours from
old masters
Dark - Brooding.

GLASGOW
Edinburgh.

65 732104

Thick paint.

early summer, when the young braves' blood was up, they took advantage of these well-lit nocturnes to ride hundreds of miles to ambush and slaughter settlers no matter their race or creed. Only by displaying valor and skill in war could they advance in tribal society, make merit, and acquire horses and wives, in that order.

Sally's transformation was complete and quite formidable. Rufus thought she even moved like a man. Only the telltale bulge of her hips and the occasional heave of her breasts gave any hint of the young female body hidden beneath homespun cloth.

Sally said nothing as they rode stirrup-to-stirrup north toward Fort Parker, the nearest white settlement. They worked to stay just under the ridge and out of sight in all the bright light. The extra horses and pack animal made little sound as they glided through the high grass, down one slope, up another.

They sensed movement around them—it was felt and heard but not yet seen. When the moon came out from behind a cloud they were amazed to find themselves in the midst of a large herd of horses and bison, their heads all down in the tall grass grazing. Rufus and Sally sat their horses in silence. With so many pintos and buffalo present, Rufus reasoned, an Indian encampment must not be far away. They rode on—up a draw and down another, the smell of wild horses, buffalo, sweat, and manure in their nostrils.

Sally still had her father's big horse pistol in her lap and, tied to her saddle, was sawed-off 16-gauge shotgun that Mr. Erstwhistle had brought back from the war. Rufus carried his Winchester barrel-down in a scabbard by his saddle, the Navy Colt pistol in his right hand resting on the pommel. He cocked it when he saw what he at first hoped was a mirage: campfires down by a river not half a mile away, and Apache teepees lit bright by the moon.

Rufus and Sally rode quietly on, away from the horses and bison. Then, clear as day, moving directly toward them at a slow, hypnotic pace, came mounted riders carrying shields and lances. If the mysterious warriors saw them, they did not acknowledge it but passed by not a dozen yards to their lee. Rufus could make out their features—they seemed taller, more erect than the Apaches. He noted their war paint—faces half-black, half-white—as they rode in the direction of the languishing herd.

Sally and Rufus sat still as death, their horses munching grass and occasionally hoofing the hard ground. Finally, they looked at each other and simultaneously spurred their mounts to a gallop, looking back over their shoulders when they heard high-pitched war cries and the sound of lances banging against rawhide shields.

The ground trembled under the quickening hooves of

the herd. The beasts thundered down the shallow valley toward the river. A stampede was under way.

The silent, war-painted riders were pushing the horses and buffalo toward the Apache camp. Sally and Rufus were witnessing a Comanche raid on their ancient, sworn blood enemies. The reservation Apaches were on the Comanches' hunting ground. As much as these ultimate Plains Indians hated the European settlers who took their land, killed their buffalo, gave them whiskey and disease, the Comanches hated the Apache more.

The rampaging herd obliterated the campfires and tepees. Rufus and Sally could see and hear the slaughter but thought it best to ride away from it all, toward their own kind. This they did in silence.

The adobe walls and stockade of Fort Parker took form in the early light. The two of them rode through the gate to gap-toothed smiles, scratched heads, and endless questions. They learned that all the soldiers, rangers, and militia were out on patrol in pursuit of the fast, agile war parties on the loose all up and down the frontier on which the Comanche Moon shone.

Sally had been nine hours in the saddle and never complained once. When she finally got down from her mare she stared straight ahead and took off her big, wide-brimmed hat. Her long blonde hair cascaded down like a waterfall. There was an audible gasp from those gathered around. She said not a word. With the early rays of light shining on her sad young face, Rufus thought her the most beautiful sight on earth—and, of course, there were those hips.

Rufus took off his hat and stood before her, not knowing what to say. She looked at him and silently mouthed the words, "Thank you." He smiled broadly, his entire future stretched out before him. They had survived in storybook fashion, and now they would thrive, together, forever in this harsh but bountiful land.

Their young eyes met again; they stared long and hard at one another. Rufus, hat in hand, shuffled his feet a bit and gave her his most expectant look.

Once again, Sally's lips parted and silently formed a word: "No."

Rufus watched the womenfolk surround Sally and take her away, intent as they were on undoing the gender transmogrification that had saved her life.

"Well, so long, Sal," he said, under his breath.

Rufus had outrun arrows, bullets, and savage rage. He had looked certain death in the face and laughed. But this rejection business was new, different, debilitating.

By rote, he began to do the one thing he knew how to do—tend livestock. He unsaddled, fed, and watered the horses, checked their hooves and legs for cuts, briars, and brambles. The purloined pack mule was the last. Rufus let the buffalo hides fall to the ground. There must've been a score of them, worth five dollars apiece in St. Louis but not much out here. There were pots, pans, and mirrors for trading with the Kiowa.

As he started to remove the harness, Rufus discovered a canvas satchel under the mule's blanket. It fell open, and a small leather pouch—like the bags squaws made for their braves to fill with magic and tie next to their testicles—landed hard on his foot.

Rufus picked up the bag and opened it. Inside was a bright-yellow, dust-like substance; it was quite heavy. The next bag held small, shiny nuggets. There must've been nigh unto a dozen of these leather bags in the satchel.

Rufus sat down on the pile of buffalo hides, the treasure trove in his lap. He was light-headed and dizzy as it finally became clear what great good fortune was this unexpected twist of fate.

He thought about Sally—just for a moment—and then lifted his head and said out loud,

"Well, I'll just be goddamned."

DIGRESSIONS
ON VITICULTURE

Romare smiled when I singled out the large glass bowl. It once held tropical fish, I suppose, but now was filled with old corks from vintage bottles of wine. Of all the souvenirs and exotic *objets d'art* collected and displayed throughout his vast mountaintop retreat, this was—to my mind—the most peculiar and compelling.

At my request, he reached into the bowl, extracted a cork, and held it up for examination. On it was written a date, *12/23/62*; a place, *Nairobi*; a star, exclamation points, an asterisk, and other marks that made for a personal hieroglyphic he alone could decode.

In a lifetime of travel and adventure, Romare Bettencourt had won considerable acclaim and countless awards for writing with insight and passion about the world's bleeding sores, exotic destinations, and the people who perpetrated and occupied them both.

His smile broke into a broad grin, then a full-bodied laugh.

"Ahhhh. The young anthropologist! Passing through

Nairobi on her way to Olduvai. She was at the Norfolk Hotel, as was I.

"Don't know if she ever discovered the origins of our species, but we both left Nairobi knowing a great deal about each other and the appetites of a sexual nature that have maintained our species at the top of the food chain for lo these countless millennia.

"What a delightful time to be in Africa," he continued. "Revolution was in the air, old Brit Colonials still stumbling about, a bit confused. Hemingway and his ilk came and went. Karen Blixen was in her dotage but still held her Old World salons at the farmhouse in the Ngong hills. It was all quite solemn and formal, yet mesmerizing for a young ex-pat with a typewriter."

"What about the anthropologist?" I inquired.

"Oh, yes. Catherine. She was a fine, compliant companion. A beautiful, decorative creature. I took her everywhere, to everything. She thrived in Nairobi, and then—poof!— she was gone."

"Have you written about this?"

"Heavens no! I would never betray a lover or friend. Haven't published in the first person, really. Also, you'll note that the wine was a Chateau Margaux 1948. Pierre Lachine. Very fine, especially with the backstrap of springbok grilled at table in the Norfolk's courtyard."

"My God, you remember all that?"

"And more, my dear child. Much, *much* more." He reached for another cork.

"Havana, 1959. I just missed Fidel at the Hotel Nacional. This was one of the last old-growth Bordeaux in their cellar. The girls of the Copa's chorus line were as giddy and anxious as they were lusty, knowing things were about to change for them—and all of Cuba. It was the only time I visited Ernest at La Finca Vigia. We were to go for billfish, but the Pilar was in dry dock. He and Mary stayed dead drunk the whole time. And paranoid? My God!"

"This is quite remarkable," I said. "Do you sit around of an evening and pull out these little time capsules of recollection?"

"No, not at all." He laughed. "I have not dipped into the deep end of this anecdotal bowl in years. It's all for your amusement. Pick one!"

I'd first met Mr. Bettencourt in journalism school. He was on a panel whose topic was "Cultural Casualties of the Cold War." He was everything my professors were not—charming, concise, convincing, and, in a word, authentic. He had been there, lived in the world, and witnessed much. Now I was here to interview him for my long overdue dissertation. It seemed to be going well.

Chateau Petrus was stamped on the cork I chose. The writing was dense and somewhat smudged. Romare studied the object as though he were deciphering Sanskrit.

"Let's see. Ah, the Land of Smiles. Bangkok's Oriental Hotel. Must have been 1957 or '58—hard to read here.

"Jim Thompson lived there before his Thai Silk business got off the ground. I knew him during the war. OSS, of course. We had a lively time.

"I recall this water festival. Loy Kratong. Always in October. Dry season but still hotter than the hinges of Hell out there. At night the Cha Phraya filled with small floating flower barges lit with candles. Otherworldly—just gorgeous! People threw coins as gifts to the deities. Children would dive after them. Some drowned every year, I was told, but the river gods must be placated."

He paused, turning the cork over in his hand, and then continued.

"There was this young man from the South—Georgia, I believe—who entered Jim's employ. He devoured the language and culture. Quite good manners. A brilliant fellow. Wrote a fine biography of Thompson after he disappeared in '67. So sad, that—"

I interrupted. "What do the other markings mean?"

"Oh, the evening was splendid—but ended strangely. After dinner, Jim had always arranged entertainments. Thai dancers. Such miniature delights—lithe and delicate and sensual in every way. They performed in small groups, then moved about amongst us. Guests would claim one or two and fade away into the anterooms, for God knows what purposes.

"The place was clearing out. It was getting late when Jim presented me with this fabulously festooned dancer in native dress. Such subservience, seductive body language, with all the bowing and wahing—very Thai. I thought, *Well, when in Bangkok....*

"I took this bottle of wine when we walked upstairs to my rooms. Very sweet, the Petrus. Thai food goes much better with beer, actually."

"Do go on, Romare!"

"The minute we got inside, without much prompting, the inevitable disrobing began. I recall the ceiling fan made this *whomp, whomp, whomp* sound. My companion lost composure only when the last garment fell to the floor. I must have looked as shocked as I was. There before me, in all of nature's glory, stood the most beautiful young boy. Eleven or twelve, I suppose. It's hard to tell with the Thais. He could have been twenty for all I know."

"Yes, and then?"

"Well, I poured myself a glass of Gallic courage and gave him one, too. In the heat of the evening he began to shiver. He'd apparently never tasted wine. It was all rather awkward. We had no common language, no cultural understanding.

"I still don't know why, but I went over to my luggage and produced two framed photographs that I always traveled with back then. Of my twins, Lars and Elizabeth. They were on a beach in Florida. Their hair sun-bleached and

blowing in the Gulf breeze, surf lapping at their thighs, faces all aglow in their own land of smiles. Timeless even now, after all these years.

"My naked dancer's black eyes grew large when he saw them. We pointed back and forth. He'd look at me, then at them. He understood, I think.

"They would have been about the same age. He couldn't take his eyes off the children and only stopped trembling when I draped a robe around his shoulders.

"We fell asleep, his head in my lap. When the sun came up, he was gone and so was one of the photographs."

A smile returned to Romare's face. He replaced the cork and looked over at me.

"He chose Liz."

As Romare left to refresh our drinks, he remarked over his shoulder, "I've a surprise for you."

The lights in his trophy room dimmed. The music, a Rachmaninoff concerto, rose a notch, and I heard the faint pop of a cork being extracted. Romare returned with two oversized crystal glasses and a dusty bottle of Burgundy. I recognized its sensuous shape, its cork on the silver tray.

"Did you bring your overnight kit? You will be staying, won't you?"

BEAT IT LIKE
IT OWES YOU MONEY

When writing, I find it impossible to concern myself with the arcane rules of spelling and punctuation. The plight of the dangling participle concerns me not at all, especially when operating under the threat of death. But syntax—that's quite another matter.

For me, writing has always come from reading. Words produce words, simple as that. Call me pitifully post-modern if you must, but that's why I am currently blocked, constipated, bound-up. I am hard-pressed to find a sustainable grouping of words in any comprehensible language on this outcropping of rocks in the middle of the Aegean in October with the Meltemi coming to an end—but more on that later.

The summer people, those formally beautiful and deliciously trashy European languishers who populate the place from May until September, are mercifully gone, including the one who is directly responsible for my current predicament.

My hostess, the ancient Lady MacWorthington, widow of Lord MacWorthington and last of the stodgy old colonials, has a library of sorts. Obscure, mostly 19th-century titles in first editions are here, but she won't let me leave the house with any. I can read all I want under her watchful eye and constant commentary and occasional hand on my thigh—she goes a little higher each day—and endless cups of black tea that run through me like the mighty Mississippi flowing unvexed to the sea.

There are some fascinatingly obscure titles that could be just the thing to catapult me into a creative/competitive state, which is crucial to my productivity and which, since I have aged, I find harder and harder to acquire. Other writers may do the same; I don't know and could not care less. I never credit my muse, and it's hardly plagiarism—more like literary drafting—when I get behind a fine, rich passage that's moving along at a fast clip, I can grab onto its cadence, its form and plot, and especially dialogue and speech patterns, and can sustain the refrain in my own words indefinitely.

I use other writing not to find my voice—I have no voice. Yet I've a career, and quite a successful one.

My personal life—my experiences, family history, emotions, and anecdotes—never make their way into my writing, but when I find myself in that word-filled wind-tunnel, the sentences just flow and flow. They seldom need editing or revision. It's magic.

But now I've lost my mojo, and that goddamn oligarch of a Russian with the 300-meter-long yacht he calls the

Obscenity has promised to forgive my debts—and there are many—and spare my life, but only if I write the most compelling piece of prose he has read in his newly acquired language, English. (Thank God I won't be competing with Tolstoy, Dostoevsky, and he who bites the hand that fed him, Solzhenitsyn.)

Serge Lutz Romanov (not his real name) plans to return to these rocky shoals in late November. "We will have Thanksgiving together," he declares, that being his new favorite holiday. I will present the fruits of my imagination, and he will decide if I live or die.

• • •

How it came about:

This was my first mistake, though I made many. The four of us—Serge and one of his fancifully named and ever-present bodyguards, Molotov or Kalashnikov or something associated with a cocktail; Winslow Malaise (his real name!), a foppish, professorial type from Antioch College on sabbatical and traveling under the aegis of the Fulbright Foundation (your tax dollars at work); and I—were sitting at the posh gaming table aboard that disgusting, floating monument to wretched excess and dysfunctional capitalism, the *Obscenity*.

Serge had picked up this Malaise (oh, I do so love the sound of that) in a bar in Monte Carlo's Grand Casino. They'd struck up a conversation about the Lost Generation—Fitzgerald, Hemingway, Dos Passos, and all the other insecure pencil-dick scribblers who had survived or dodged the Great War and just felt awful about it.

During one of my brandy-fueled diatribes aimed at the effete and feckless Malaise, I cavalierly dismissed the whole lot, especially Fitzgerald, who couldn't recognize a good thing when he found one—Zelda, Hollywood, fame and fortune (if fleeting), rakish good looks, et cetera.

I came down especially hard on *The Crack-Up*, his sketchy autobiographical piece about mental instability published in that paragon of lofty intellectualism, *Esquire* magazine (circa 1936). Such whining and complaining, so weak and lily-livered.

"Be a man," says I, followed by: "He gave permission to a whole phalanx of confessional writers—the contemptible Robert Lowell, the boring Ann Beatty, and that whole miserable, navel-gazing, MFA-grasping crowd that still occupies to a great extent America's literary landscape."

Malaise was nodding off and about to fall out of his overstuffed leather chair when Serge raised the pot €10,000 and gave me one of his signature squinty-eyed, Cossack stares.

"And you can do better?" he queried.

"Ha! Of course!" I shot back. "With one blind eye, the other bloodshot, and my writing hand tied behind me. I am a professional!"

"Well," said Serge, "the mutilation of the eye won't be necessary, unless of course you do not win. I like a good wager, especially when something dear is at stake. I look forward to reading your response, your treatise."

"I beg your pardon?" I gasped. "Are you proposing a bet of some kind?"

"Yes, of course. All of your debts will be forgiven and the *Obscenity* will take you around the world if you win. If you lose, well—" He pulled a finger across his throat.

My pickled brain tried to make sense of this. "How will we know? Who will judge?"

"Why, Professor Malaise here. He has a PhD from Princeton," Serge announced with an unearned lilt of Ivy League arrogance.

"Which should disqualify him," I sputtered. "Fitzgerald went to Princeton. They deify him there. Malaise can hardly be objective."

It was all for naught. The Fulbright fellow's head was flat on the table and stirred only when Serge offered him a €10,000 fee for "literary consultation."

The *Obscenity* would weigh anchor on the morrow. Malaise would stay on board to give tutorials on 20th-century American Lit until Serge, the *Obscenity,* and its entourage returned for the ultimate read-off.

We parted in cold silence. One thing was very clear. Should my offering not match or exceed Fitzgerald, it was lights out, so long, *sayonara,* sweet dreams, *adios, arrivederci,* the Big Sleep *pour moi!*

· · ·

This I knew. My nemesis had not come by his wealth passively. He had killed before, readily, and even bragged about it. After the collapse of the Soviet Union there'd been a mad scramble for assets among Russia's would-be oligarchs. Serge Romanov and Molotov/Kalashnikov/Baryshnikov had duked it out with a small army of former Soviet intelligence officers intent on taking oil and mining interests that were a huge part of Serge's empire. There had been casualties, and Serge would have been among them except for Molotov/Smirnoff (or whatever his goddamn name was), who had snatched Serge's chestnuts from the fire. The two were devoted to one another, and Serge was seldom out Molotov's sight.

For all of his high-profile wealth and acquisitions, Serge had powerful enemies. Now, as one of the last men standing, our not-so-benevolent host did not cotton to being challenged, contradicted, or made to look the slightest bit foolish, and unfortunately his English was getting better.

As I slowly came to my senses, I began to calculate my chances. Winslow Malaise had read my work in obscure literary journals and *The New York Review of Books* and claimed to have admired a *New York Times* Op-Ed on Third World writers and why they mattered. He had not read my novels or my memoir, which was probably a good thing.

He did, however, fondly recall a *New Yorker* piece praising a resurgent interest in William Faulkner and why his prose soared in such a singular way, occupying a stratosphere all its own, with no need for the unnecessary burden of punctuation.

It occurred to me: Malaise could be finessed and would certainly have a say, but Serge would have the final word on whether I lived or died. I did not plan to go gently into that good night.

Turkey Day was a mere six weeks away. If I was not to be the one roasted, I must eventually get back to Lady MacWorthington's musty library, open my thighs, make amends, and put on a charm offensive to all I had offended—and there had been many.

I agonized for weeks on end. When I next called on the Grande Dame, I found by the door a stack of old books (are there any other kind?) to be donated to the Red Cross. When I reached down, fate filled my hand with a copy of *Big Woods*, a 1937 edition of William Faulkner's hunting stories. Faulkner! What was it about this tiny man with the outsized vision?

I met him, you know, in the winter of 1962, at West Point. That's right—I was destined for a military career but instead followed in the path of such distinguished dropouts as J.M. Whistler and E.A. Poe, who both fled that fortress on the Hudson as soon as they could flunk out. But one February morning, in my English class, reading from his work, was William Faulkner along with Henri Cartier-Bresson, who was busy snapping photographs. There is one of the Great Man and me; his high-pitched voice haunts me still.

I took the book, better destined for *moi* than some encephalitic, terminal patient in the local infirmary. I read and reread it. Copied the text, typing word-for-word *The Bear, The Old People, Race at Morning*, even the dedication to Faulkner's editor, Saxe Cummins:

> We never always saw eye to eye
> but we were always
> looking at the same thing

Brilliant!

It was the introduction that encapsulated and held fast his native place, Mississippi, from prehistory to the present. You could see the timeless landscape, smell the humid air and fresh blood. It was all there, and I was captivated. Here was genius on the page. Nothing lost about this man, his generation notwithstanding.

I recalled that Serge Romanov had become emotional only once in my presence—when he and Molotov laughed and sobbed deep into the night, an empty vodka bottle between them, about the ancient village on the Russian Steppes from whence these two unlikely survivors sprung.

That's it!

I will substitute all things Russian for all things Faulkner—the Volga for the Mississippi, Cossacks for Choctaws, serfs for slaves, bear for bear, and on and on.

Praise the Lord.

I am saved—or so I hoped.

It was the morning before Thanksgiving, and the Meltemi, that ill wind from the north, was having one last blow. It is said the Macedonian King Philip planned his military campaigns in sync with the predictable Meltemi to keep enemy ships at bay. That was too much for me to ask, but I did sense a good omen with every breeze.

The sleek profile of the *Obscenity* appeared on the horizon, drew closer, and dropped anchor. Serge, Malaise, and a dozen of his Euro-trash hangers-on came ashore in the launch operated by the ever-present Molotov/Smirnoff/ Popov. We had drinks at a seaside bar. I was unusually calm compared to the weather when Serge asked, "So, my friend, are you ready for your trial by words? To put Hemingway, Fitzgerald, and the entire Lost Generation in their place?"

"I am prepared," I replied with Zen-like composure.

It was all arranged. The launch would return for me tomorrow at 5:00 p.m. We would have a sumptuous meal, the Filipino staff was to dress as Pilgrims and Indians, and then I would state my case.

I slept well that night. Next afternoon, girding my loins

for battle, I fastened my vintage Patek Phillipe watch to my left wrist and knotted a silk Ferragamo tie in a half-Windsor snug against the collar of my Turnbull & Asser shirt, sleeves held fast by Clinton-era presidential cufflinks. I slipped on white cotton Saville Row slacks, added a bespoke blazer, a Burberry of London scarlet square flowering from its breast pocket. Gucci loafers—no socks, of course. I put on my polarized Ray-Ban sunglasses, collected the leather Louis Vuitton valise that contained the key to my questionable future—ten pages of typescript—and started for the pier, some one-hundred paces from my quarters.

The *Obscenity* was backlit by the setting sun in a most dramatic fashion. The launch and the ever-dependable Ivan Novaya Molotovski (I had at long last learned his name) were idling just off the dock. I walked to the end, waved, and shouted to get his attention. He glanced my way, looked back at the *Obscenity*, then at his watch.

At that very moment the great ship's hull seemed to inflate and lift out of the water. A bright-orange fireball engulfed the *Obscenity*, blinding all except those wearing Ray-Bans. The sound and concussion reached us an instant later. It knocked me to earth and forced the launch hard up against the pier.

I sat up and looked directly at Molotovski, not ten meters away. Smiling, he raised a thumb to his front teeth and flipped a timeless (if lower-class) gesture of disdain, disgust, and dismissal. Then Molotovski opened the throttle and motored off.

I was stunned but regained my feet and composure. The great ship and all it stood for were gone, disappeared, vanished like a bad dream. My leather valise had come open and the neatly typed pages were swirling around my feet and into the water.

It was Thanksgiving and, at long last, I had something to be thankful for.

365-0246
Friday Night
6 P.M.
Versailles
"the Golden mean"
Golden mean
2 Nd Light Left
Building

Feel free to make your own sketches here

Feel free to make your own sketches here

Afterword

WILLIAM DUNLAP is not like you and me. I've always known that his wit was quicker, his pen and brush abler, his take on the world funnier than almost anyone else's. What I didn't know is that this self-styled Southern-gentleman/rock-star character—this blue-eyed, fashion-forward, keenly observant, gallant, sharp-tongued, thoughtful, peripatetic, laughing, brooding, always-intense artist—had it in him to be a writer of starkly arresting fiction.

Billy is full of opposites. He is at once a hedonist and a stoic, entertainer and introvert, satirist and social worker. He is as loyal a friend as it is possible to be, and yet a more mercurial, independent man would be hard to find. It is difficult to think of a more devoted husband and father—in the same skin as this restless, roving, adventure-seeking critic of the universe. He functions literally as a critic on public television, opining on selected artists and their exhibitions, but rarely does he bring a liverish or dismissive tone to his pronouncements. In the public arena he tends to be resolutely upbeat, favoring the celebratory and the encouraging. In private he can be counted on to bring a biting, even lacerating perspective to any discussion. His dismissals or scabrous jokes at someone else's expense are delivered, however, somehow impersonally and in an atmosphere of the light, passing jibe. The darkness beneath the generosity is only subtly glimpsed.

So now we have these stories. They stand on their own as bitter little parables: hilarious narratives of nubile innocence and its natural potential for depredation; fables of vanity and of the joys and perils of dandyish self-importance that Oscar Wilde would recognize as his very meat. Jonathan Swift is hardly more acid in his indictments of institutional depravity than Dunlap taking on the Church in "Fable of the Holy See"; and who, including Bill's acquaintance Tom Wolfe, has more pointedly skewered the kitschy heart of America's decadent elite than he does in "A Life Well Lived"? Sometimes the writer summons his own experience (we glimpse the subversive schoolboy in the classroom), and we can imagine his witnessing a scene in a Waffle House not so different from that in "Open All Night." More often he weaves his parables with threads from the countless movies and histories and other lore of World War II ("WHAM! BAM! POW!") that a curious and literate Southern lad inevitably made his own. Dunlap has always harbored a fascination for the romantic, twentieth-century paradigm of the heroic-yet-sensitive, virile, erudite, adventurous sexual and cultural pioneer. Jack London and John Steinbeck and Ernest Hemingway and Isak Dinesen created chivalric legends that will live forever in Bill's heart; Walker Percy and Hunter S. Thompson created hyper-realistic myths that are lodged in his gut. And of course he would have to have been led to the great American entrepreneur and adventurer Jim Thompson—savior of the Thai textile industry in the mid-twentieth century, raconteur, catalyst for generations of Western seekers and sensualists in Thailand— whose legend and reality seem to have pierced Dunlap to the core. Still, with "Digressions on Viticulture," he proves that even his most sanctified subjects are not immune to a skewering from his bird's-eye vantage, which sees the fatuousness of everything self-dramatizing. He turns the things he most loves into fodder for ridicule and then redeems them with *tours de force* of sheer comic brilliance.

These stories need no illustration from the artist's adroit pen. And yet they are comfortably juxtaposed here with his parallel world of visual meanderings. As a longtime consumer of Dunlap's visual art, I have often been more responsive to the intricacies of his small-scale drawings than to the narrative macrocosms of the larger painting compositions. When the two are in harmony, the paintings work effortlessly; when, in the paintings, discordant or disconnected elements occur, they are sometimes diminished and sometimes made more compelling. Even when the imagery is indigestible, the artist has generally insisted on presenting highly finished, worked-through compositions rather than informal doodlings or ideas in progress. But now, with this publication, it is possible to experience the prodigiousness of Dunlap's wrist in some less-calculated, less-finished meanderings with pen and pencil. As a painter, he has stubbornly hewed to a fundamentally conservative tradition in terms of medium, technique, format, and style. He is part of a thread in American art that includes both Winslow Homer and Andrew Wyeth. What separates his paintings and drawings decisively from those more literal, earlier artists is an undercurrent of violence or dread or loss. This quality connects his visual work to many of his southern compatriots in the realms of poetry and literature. Dunlap is emphatically not a bucolic, or *plein air,* painter. He is a studio artist, a pure inventor. Every work comes from a narrative that springs from the artist's cumulative preoccupations, filtered through his often-vexed imagination.

Now suddenly we are called upon to evaluate and contextualize these strange stories. It is impossible not to make a few literary comparisons. It seems obvious that most of his resonances are to other Southern writers. I think of the at least partially Southern-associated Donald Barthelme, or John Kennedy Toole, perhaps inescapably of Flannery O'Conner. In Dunlap's case, one needn't just speculate about other writers whose work he might have read—several major figures are, or were, good friends:

Gore Vidal, Willie Morris, Barry Hannah, Lee Smith, Winston Groom; historians and memoirists Shelby Foote and Howell Raines; the poets James Dickey, John Foster West, Jonathan Williams—all have been significantly present in his life. He has made the acquaintance of Eudora Welty; he was practically baptized in the myth and magic of William Faulkner. He reads and reads. All of this context may help place the tenor of these short pieces of Bill's, but it doesn't explain them. They seem to come from a place of pure, distilled imagination—a sort of remembering of things that, just because they happened in dreams, are no less true and immediate than what happens in "real life."

Until recently, however, he has not (as far as we knew) written. He is, in his words, a "self-diagnosed dyslexic. Without the technology of Siri, where I can dictate and play around, these stories wouldn't exist." This is an important fact. We are well acquainted with painters and sculptors who could barely read (Dunlap himself cites the severe dyslexia of one of his heroes, Robert Rauschenberg). We are not, however, so familiar with a powerfully right-brained individual who can put words together in quite the tightly woven, forward-propelled, rhythmic fashion of the rascally little fables we have here. The rhythmic part might be associated with the fact that, among his many attributes, Bill Dunlap is no mean drummer. He has played with various bands at various times in his life, always finding the task natural and unforced. A lot of things that come easily to the right-brained wunderkind don't to the left-brained intellectual. In Bill's case, the secret may be a deceptively obvious one. He is a fast-talking and highly articulate gentleman whose gifts and aspirations as a painter help him define himself. He is also a self-described performer, with and without a drum set—he has even referred to himself as a "performance artist." We think of him as a reliably funny, generous, and entertaining friend.

What we also unconsciously know but don't always remember about William Dunlap is that he is perhaps the most attentive, porous listener/observer it is possible to be. How can someone who talks and reacts and creates so much also be imbibing so much? Sometimes the mask descends for a moment, and Bill's attention is directed inward, or we become aware that the words are being emitted while the brain is absorbing something in another part of the room. We know not only from observation that the listening is happening but also because the wellspring of references and memories is so vast. We also now and then sense the mood of secret cogitation, occasionally of uneasiness or melancholy, that can underlie the performance. The ever-present if deeply buried introvert peers out and, for a brief moment, reveals himself. It is a mysterious thing, this porous receptivity and retention and genius for recreation, especially in one whose external persona is so gloriously perfected. It may be that this quality of heightened listening is the key to the artist. The language—the voice—that we can now suddenly read and thus hear, coming from the place of retention and reflection, offers a whole new point of entry for our appreciation of this inimitable man.

—Jane Livingston

FLINT HILL, VIRGINIA

Postage Stamp of Native soil

Broom sage

Broom sage

Pool

Acknowledgements

LINDA BURGESS, mother of our daughter, Maggie, and the finest line editor I know with the best eye and ear in this family.

Ron Goldfarb, author, agent, and bulldog lawyer whose tolerance for the Southern voice and temperament is matched only by his own many works of fact and fiction.

All early readers of Short Mean Fiction—you know who you are and what I put you through.

Ken DeCell, a son of the Mississippi Delta who edits in his sleep and in life is a first-rate rock 'n' roller and singer of medieval motets.

John Langston, who is as yet unsullied by the Ivy League and has brought untold beauty, order, elegance, and pleasure to our universe.

Neil White, visionary and fearless (he's married to a divorce lawyer!) publisher who took a flyer on *SMF*—a lapse in judgment we hope will not be fatal.

Jane Livingston, friend and confidante of long standing who knows all there is to know. (I know the rest.) We live to please her.

Steven Goodwin, whose writing I so admire and whose insight and enthusiasm for these tales was sustaining.

Billy Friedkin, there is no one at all like him. Artist, auteur, author and American original whose realism, while not for everyone, is in fact the ONLY one.

Ed McGowin, Golden Gloves champ and aesthetic polevaulter who set the bar high for us all.

Pat Oliphant, consummate artist and curmudgeon from an early age, whose concept Saint Pedophilia was. I owe him much.

Carolyn Evans, easy to look at and listen to, and with a steel trap of a mind.

Steve Yarbrough, another Delta picker and master of language, who told what many suspect to be true about World War II.

The late and lamented Barry Hannah, fellow traveler and unapologetic Mississippian who rose to the top tier of MC's BSU prayer list, as did I.

Julia Reed, astute, insightful, and inspired chronicler of the passing human parade. She sees all there is to see and is the original SWMBO (She Who Must Be Obeyed) and I comply.

Carol Harrison, artist and photographer whose gathering of artist portraits is unmatched, meaningful and unstinting. We are the way she sees us.

Jim Kimsey—from a high cliff in the Grenadines we

both glimpsed the world's largest yacht which became, in my mind's eye, the *Obscenity*.

John Alexander, the best pure painter I know and a social, psychological, and pathological force of nature.

Sally Mann says it all in *Hold Still* and whose focus is constant. She is the best we have.

R.T. "Rod" Smith, poet and Blue Ridge Mountain cohort from way back; a great lover of life and art who respects them both.

The late Black Mountain poet Jonathan Williams, who made books like most people make biscuits.

John Saltmarsh, Kings College historian and archivist in whose company I spent a memorable afternoon in July 1974.

Monsignor Paul Canonice, painter, patrician, and Delta Italian of the first order.

Jim Roche, a self-described "outhouse Southerner" who nonetheless is the finest artist of our generation.

T.R. Fehrenbach, whose matchless writing about the west and Plains Indians I find galvanizing.

William Warren, our man in Bangkok, who still has and exercises "beautiful manners." His biography of Jim Thompson is perfection on the page.

And of course there is Siri, my digital interlocutor, whose tendency to auto-correct often makes sentences more colorful if less comprehensible.

William Dunlap – 2015
In the studio at work on Beautiful Dreamer,
charcoal drawing of Eudora Welty.

Photograph by Carol Harrison